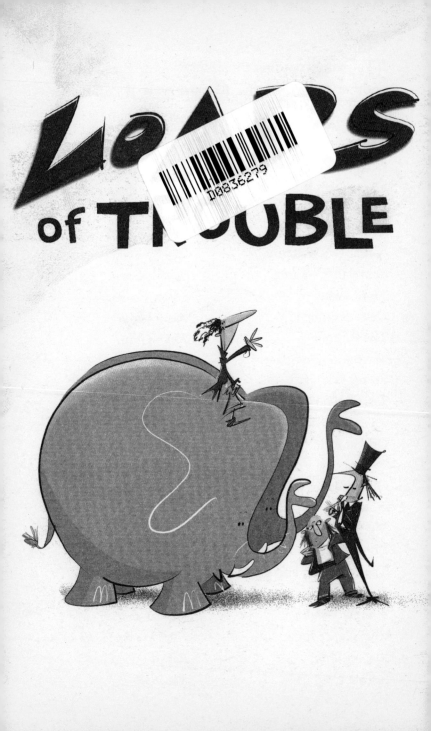

If you enjoy reading this book, you might like to try another story from the **MAMMOTH READ** series:

Carly's Luck	*Rachel Anderson*
Esme's Owl	*William Bedford*
Dolphin Boy	*Julie Bertagna*
Name Games	*Theresa Breslin*
Little Elephant	*W.J. Corbett*
Forbidden Memories	*Jamila Gavin*
Someone's Watching, Someone's Waiting	*Jamila Gavin*
Time Swing	*Pippa Goodhart*
Dead Trouble	*Keith Gray*
The Runner	*Keith Gray*
More Jessame Stories	*Julia Jarman*
Secret Friends	*Pete Johnson*
Tiny the Terrier	*Linda Kempton*
The Gargoyle	*Garry Kilworth*
On the Run	*Elizabeth Laird*
Swapper	*Robert Leeson*
Ghost Blades	*Anthony Masters*
How's Harry	*Steve May*
My Frog and I	*Jan Mark*
The Winter Wolf	*Lynne Markham*
The Sandman and the Turtles	*Michael Morpurgo*
Delilah and the Dogspell	*Jenny Nimmo*
Tommy Trouble	*Stephen Potts*
Chocolate Magic	*Patrick Skene Catling*
Roger's War	*Robert Swindells*
If Cats Could Fly	*Robert Westall*

Andrew Matthews

LOADS of TROUBLE

Illustrated by **Tony Ross**

mammoth

First published in Great Britain 1991
by Methuen Children's Books Ltd
Published 1993 by Mammoth
Reissued 2000 by Mammoth
an imprint of Egmont Children's Books Limited,
a division of Egmont Holding Limited,
239 Kensington High Street, London W8 6SA

ISBN 0 7497 0660 0

10 9 8 7 6 5 4 3

A CIP catalogue record for this title
is available from the British Library

Printed and bound in Great Britain
by Cox & Wyman Ltd, Reading, Berkshire

Contents

To Bob, Jill, Miriam and David

ONE

A Nuisance

Lady Feeblerick was the most refined person in seven counties. She drank her afternoon tea from a cup of the finest bone china. The milk in her milk jug was whiter than a polar bear's bottom. The sugar cubes in her sugar bowl were polished every morning until they were dazzling. While drinking her tea, it was Lady Feeblerick's habit to leaf idly through volumes of French verse – though she didn't understand a word of French. 'That way,' she confided to a friend, 'I can avoid the possibility of reading anything vulgar.'

Lady Feeblerick was a tall slender woman, with skin like marble and eyes of such a pale grey as to appear colourless. She always dressed in white and dyed her hair the same colour until age whitened it naturally.

'Hair of any other colour would clash with my gowns,' she told her hairdresser, 'and

that would be unthinkably unrefined!'

Lady Feeblerick lived in Feeblerick Hall, a fine mansion close to the village of Chewlow. Her contact with the village went no further than opening the summer fête every August – so it came as a surprise when, one spring morning, Prudence the maid announced that a visitor from the village wanted to speak to her ladyship.

'A visitor from the village?' asked Lady

Feeblerick, in a voice like ice tinkling in a glass. 'What manner of visitor?'

'Please, m'lady, it's Mr Earwacker, chairman of the parish council,' replied Prudence with a bobbing curtsey. 'He insists that it's urgent!'

'He may be shown in,' frowned Lady Feeblerick,' 'but be sure that he wipes his boots properly!'

Moments later, Councillor Earwacker entered, clutching a curly-brimmed bowler hat to his chest. He was a plump man with a grey moustache that looked like a cringing whippet. His head was almost bald and his face was as pink and glossy as a strawberry lollipop.

'How d'you do, m'lady,' he began. 'I'll waste no time beating about the bush. You're a busy woman and I'm a busy man. I've never been one for shilly-shallying around. I was brought up to be plain-spoken and I like others to be plain-spoken in their turn. So, without further ado, I'll come straight to the point.'

Here, Councillor Earwacker paused and tapped his fingers against the brim of his bowler in what Lady Feeblerick judged to be a common manner.

9

'And what, pray, Councillor Earwacker, *is* the point?'

'It's your elephants, m'lady,' Councillor Earwacker said gravely. 'They're causing a public nuisance and the parish council has authorised me to come and see you about it.'

'My good man,' snapped Lady Feeblerick, 'elephants have been kept at the Hall ever since my dear-departed papa developed a weakness for them while taking a tropical tour. I fail to see why, after twenty years, they should suddenly be a nuisance. Have they been trumpeting at night and keeping the villagers awake?'

'No, m'lady.'

'Have they rifled fruit from the local orchards?' enquired Lady Feeblerick.

'Er, no, m'lady.'

'Perhaps,' Lady Feeblerick suggested with a touch of melodrama, 'they have run amok and trampled some residents?'

'It's not that, m'lady,' said Councillor Earwacker with a smile that made his cringing moustache twitch. 'In a word, it's droppings!'

The sound of the word 'droppings' was so shocking that Lady Feeblerick's face went the colour of whipped cream.

'Droppings?' she echoed in disbelief.

'You know – elephant muck!' said Councillor Earwacker, warming to his theme. 'Dung!'

'Councillor,' whispered Lady Feeblerick, 'will you have the kindness to call my maid? I am about to faint.'

And so saying, Lady Feeblerick drifted to the carpet like a leaf falling in autumn.

When Prudence discovered what had happened, her eyes flashed furiously. 'You are a clumsy great clot and no mistake!' she told the councillor as she wafted a bottle of smelling salts under Lady Feeblerick's nose. 'Fancy using a word like "dung" in front of a refined lady like her!'

'But that's what I came to talk about!' Councillor Earwacker protested. 'It's elephant dung that's causing the nuisance! There's a great steaming pile of it behind the elephant house! There's not a spot in Chewlow it can't be seen from and it's getting bigger every day! And it's not only the look of it! When the wind's in from the south-east, the smell gets so bad all the dogs start howling. We get flies and all sorts in the summer. Amos the apothecary says it's a real health risk! The new parish council wants to

11

put Chewlow on the map. We want to see plenty of tourists here, spending money in the shops. We want to see big companies building factories in the countryside – but who's going to want to come to a place where there's a mound of elephant manure stinking the place out? There's a deal of money to be made out of Chewlow and, at the moment, those elephants and their muck are standing in the way!'

'I'm sure I don't know about such things!' Prudence replied curtly. 'But you'll not be able to explain anything to her ladyship unless you find a way of mending your words!'

'But how can I?' cried the councillor. 'When all's said and done, dung's *dung!*'

'Shh!' urged Prudence. 'She's coming round!'

Lady Feeblerick was unable to continue her interview with Councillor Earwacker until she had been arranged on a *chaise longue* and given a glass of soda water to sip.

'Councillor,' she said hoarsely, her eyes closed in distaste, 'go on with what you were saying, but I must insist that you moderate your language!'

'Well, m'lady, the village has got a problem with your . . . er . . .' Councillor Earwacker cast about for words like a man trying to find his slippers in a dark bedroom. At last, inspiration struck him and made his eyes go glittery. 'The village has got a problem with your elephant unmentionables, m'lady!' he announced.

TWO

Toby and Bat

While Councillor Earwacker was in conference with Lady Feeblerick, the Hall elephants, Rita and Nancy, were being mucked out by their two keepers.

Rita was slightly the larger of the elephants and was the more mischievous. There was always a wicked glint in her eye and she liked to play tricks on her keepers. She hid their pitchforks underneath the straw and tweaked their bottoms with her trunk when they bent over to find them.

Nancy was a little more stately than Rita – though not by much. She browsed with great delicacy through a bale of hay, selecting the choicest morsels and carrying them to her mouth. She remembered her manners and grunted her thanks to the keepers from time to time.

The head keeper was Toby Hoken, a rather

rascally old chap with disreputable whiskers and a weakness for ale. Every day, as he cleared up after the elephants with a pitchfork, shovel and wheelbarrow, he made the same joke.

'I been round elephants these last ten years,' he wheezed, 'and elephants 'ave been all round me!' And if no one else laughed at his joke, Toby laughed at it himself, making a noise like a punctured accordion.

Because he was ancient, Toby had been provided with an apprentice, Bat. Bat had curly dark hair and eyes that were almost black. He had arrived at Feeblerick Hall one stormy night, asking for work. Nobody knew where he had come from, he simply turned up on the doorstep of the servants' entrance and what with the lashing rain, rolling thunder and crackling lightning, nobody had had the heart to turn him away. An experimental fortnight working with Toby Hoken and the elephants had lengthened into a year. Rita and Nancy adored Bat at first sight and snuffled him with their trunks whenever he came near. He was so good at getting the animals to do what he wanted that it made Toby chuckle in admiration.

'Sometimes, Bat,' the old man often told

him, 'I could swear that you spoke to them 'uge, dumb beasts in their own language!'

When Toby said this, Bat would not reply but would turn his head away and smile to himself secretly.

Just when the mucking out, feeding and watering were finished Bat noticed an unfamiliar figure approaching along the path that led up to the Hall.

'Who's this coming, Mr Hoken?' he asked.

Toby squinted and shaded his eyes. He saw sunlight gleaming on the braided waistcoat, satin breeches and powdered wig of Dawkin, her ladyship's footman.

'That,' Toby told Bat with a sly chuckle, 'is as puffed-up and precious a popinjay as ever preened!'

The footman reached the end of the path and began a windy journey across the yard to avoid soiling his shiny pumps.

'Oh, ain't 'e a picture!' gurgled Toby. 'Cuter than a Yule log! 'E wants to watch someone don't come up be'ind 'im with a sprig of 'olly!'

At length, Dawkin reached the end of his travels and stood before Toby and Bat with a face as long and stuck-up as a pulpit. His clothes gave off a strong scent of violets.

'Well, Mr Dawkin?' Toby said cheerily. 'What brings you round these parts?'

Dawkin raised his right hand to his mouth, coughed and replied in a voice like a squeaking floorboard, 'Her ladyship sends you her compliments and would be obliged if you would come and see her at your earliest convenience.'

'Why's that then?' murmured Toby.

'Her ladyship, of course, confided nothing

to me,' said Dawkin, 'but I do hear tell that it concerns elephant unmentionables.'

'What the Beelzebub is elephant unmentionables?' hooted Toby.

'If you take two steps backwards,' said Dawkin, pointing to the floor of the elephant house, 'you'll not only find out what it is, you'll find yourself standing in it!'

Toby and Bat looked behind them, puzzled, then Toby burst into gravelly laughter. 'O-o-h! You mean elephant – !'

'I mean elephant unmentionables,' Dawkin interrupted hastily. 'And I'd get a move on if I were you. Her ladyship is not sunnily disposed today!'

THREE

Waldo Faldo

Dawkin had been right about Lady Feeblerick's mood. In all his years of service, Toby had never seen her look so flustered. Bat kept close to Toby's right shoulder and tried not to be overawed by his first really close look at her ladyship.

Just as intriguing as Lady Feeblerick was the man who stood beside her, holding hands with himself. He was a long and bony man with a primrose yellow waistcoat, grey suit and shoes and hair that was as slick and black as an eel. He had a curled moustache and a smile that oozed across his face like a stain spreading over a tablecloth.

'Hoken.' Lady Feeblerick nodded in greeting. 'Who's that you've got with you?'

'This is Bat, my 'prentice, ma'am,' Toby explained.

'Do you think it entirely proper for the boy

to be named after a flying nocturnal mammal?' demanded Lady Feeblerick.

'Well, ma'am,' said Toby, with a twinkle in his eye, "'e's rightly called Bartholemew, but it's such a long name that when I tried to say it, I kept slippin' off the end and bruisin' my shins, so I shortened it to Bat!'

Lady Feeblerick blinked at Toby as coolly as an Arctic fish. 'Stop your nonsense and listen to me, Hoken! People in the village have made complaints about the elephants.'

'Ah!' grinned Toby. 'Them and their unmentionables, is it?'

Lady Feeblerick ignored Toby's grin and pressed on.

'This is a serious matter, Hoken. The parish council have served me with an order to get rid of what they call the elephant pollution problem.'

'We could always stop feedin' 'em, ma'am!' quipped Toby. 'That ought to do the trick!' His shoulders quaked with silent laughter.

Bat, however, saw danger in Lady Feeblerick's eyes and there was something about the face of the oily stranger that made him want to shudder.

'Hoken,' Lady Feeblerick said, 'the council have given me no choice. If no answer can be found to the problem within a week, the elephants will have to go.'

Mirth left Toby faster than a hamster on a wheel.

'Go, ma'am?' he croaked. "Ow d'you mean, go?'

'Perhaps your ladyship will permit me to explain,' offered the stranger, wrinkling up the corners of his eyes and spreading his smile a little wider. 'In the event of no other solution being found, the council have engaged me to make an agreement with Lady Feeblerick that will allow me to take the elephants off her hands.' He spread his own hands. They didn't look strong enough to take the skin off a satsuma.

'And who might you be, then?' Toby demanded gruffly.

'I am Waldo Faldo,' the man proclaimed. 'I am a purveyor of top-quality animal food products.'

'What d'you mean, animal food products?' puzzled Toby.

'It's quite simple,' explained Waldo Faldo smoothly, 'if the elephant problem is not solved within seven days, the council will issue a writ compelling her ladyship to sell the animals to me.'

'Is that so?' scoffed Toby. 'And what would you do with Rita and Nancy then, eh?'

Waldo Faldo bared his white teeth in a smile that would have made a cat fluff up its tail.

'I would turn them into cats' meat,' he said.

FOUR

Dead Elephant Meat

Toby Hoken leaned against the gate of the elephant house and made no attempt to wipe away the tears that streamed down his face like rain sliding down a window. The elephants, sensing that something was wrong, made sympathetic humphing noises. Rita placed her trunk around his shoulders and Nancy poked her trunk into his pocket, found a handkerchief and used it to wipe away his tears.

'I'll be flustered, flummoxed and fandangoed!' groaned Toby.

He was so depressed, he didn't notice, at first, that someone was tapping his arm. It was Bat, holding out a mug of hot tea. The mug was shaped like an elephant's head with a trunk for a handle.

'Drink this, Mr Hoken,' said Bat. 'It'll warm you and cheer you up again!'

Bat's eyes sparkled as he spoke, and some of the sparkle must have got into the tea, somehow, for after the first slurp, Toby's tears dried and the world seemed to turn more grey than black.

'I dunno, Bat! I'll be jointed, jinxed and jiggered if I know what to do! I've racked my brains so much, I think I've stretched 'em permanent!'

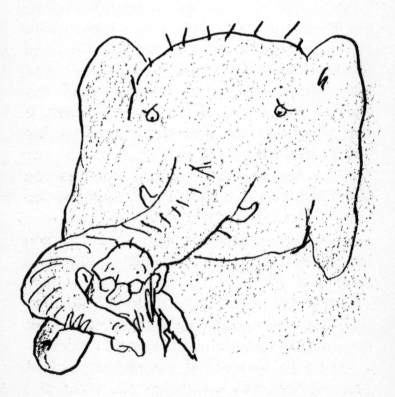

'Don't worry, Mr Hoken!' Bat said. 'We'll think of something before the week's end, you'll see!' A strange light came into his face as he spoke, but Toby took another swig of his tea and didn't notice.

'I dunno what the world's comin' to, I'm sure!' grumbled the old man. 'Once upon a time innocent creatures went about their lives just a-doin' what came natural and no one thought anythin' about it! Nowadays it's all nuisance and pollution and councils and by-laws and regulations! You can't whistle in the street without breakin' some daft rule or other!' Toby looked at the elephants and new tears squeezed out of his eyes. ''Course, if you wears a fancy suit and you got a big factory that's makin' lot's o' money, you can make as much mess and foul smell as you like! But if you're a poor dumb elephant you gets taken away and turned into cats' meat!'

'Don't upset yourself, Mr Hoken!' urged Bat. 'They haven't got the better of us yet! As soon as – '

The sound of footsteps made Bat break off and look round. The light went out of his eyes and left them looking like cold cinders.

Waldo Faldo strutted across the yard. A grey top hat was set on his oily locks at a

27

raffish angle. He had a silver-topped cane under his arm and he was dabbing his nose with a scrap of fancy silk handkerchief. There was a look of distaste on his face.

'How can you possibly bear the ghastly smell?' he enquired. 'You should thank heaven that you're so unrefined and your sense of smell is not as acute as mine!'

'Can I help you, sir?' Bat asked.

'Yes, by stepping aside,' said Waldo Faldo. 'I've come to examine the merchandise.'

Bat moved back without a word and let the glistening businessman take his place beside Toby. Waldo Faldo took out a pencil, a notebook and a little wooden slide-rule.

'Oh, yes!' he exclaimed as he looked at the elephants and calculated. His pencil point scurried across the page like a startled mouse. 'Plenty of meat there! Plenty of fat to make candles, plenty of oil for lamps! Plenty of bones for dogs and skin for shoes and suitcases. I'll have their feet turned into umbrella stands and their tails made into horsewhips! Oh, yes! There's plenty of profit here for me!'

The tone of his voice made the elephants rumble uneasily and shift their feet. Rita raised her tail to add to the pollution problem and Waldo Faldo twisted his face in revulsion. 'How disgusting!' he hissed. 'The

bigger the animal, the viler its habits, I always think!' He repocketed his writing implements and nudged Toby with a bony elbow. 'I wager you'll be glad to get shot of these monsters, eh, old-timer? You look about ready for retirement. I reckon the old girl will see you all right – she's a soft touch for all her la-di-da airs and graces!' His voice dropped to the greasiest of whispers. 'Tell you what, you walk these elephants into the slaughter-house for me, nice and quiet and I'll slip you a couple of golden guineas. What do you say to that?'

Toby was within a whisker of dashing his tea into Waldo Faldo's face, when Bat suddenly intruded.

'Mr Hoken's a bit tired at the moment, sir,' he said, smooth as double cream. 'Come and talk to me about the matter later on in the week.'

Waldo Faldo brought a black cheroot out of a silver case.

'Oh, so that's the game, is it?' He smiled slyly, lit a match with a flick of his thumbnail and applied the flame to the end of the cheroot. 'If you want to make the extra cash, that's between you and the old man. All I care about is dead elephant meat.' Waldo

Faldo drew on his cheroot until it glowed like the winking of a greedy red eye and set off across the yard.

Toby and Bat watched him go. The old man's hands trembled with rage, but Bat's voice was cool and calm.

'Don't you fret now, Mr Hoken! Waldo Faldo has taken on more than he bargained for, you see if he hasn't!'

The strange light was back in Bat's eyes as he spoke.

FIVE

Elephant Cart

The next morning, Feeblerick Hall was more agog than a trainful of monkeys in a banana plantation. There had been a most peculiar occurrence. A cart had appeared on the front drive overnight – a real monster of a four-wheeler painted red and yellow and green. No one had heard it arrive and no word of explanation had been given to anybody.

Simon Weatherby, her ladyship's coachman, was called on to give his opinion. He spent a long time walking around the cart, eyeing it intently.

'This is a big cart,' he concluded. 'In fact, it's an enormous, gigantic cart. It's the biggest one I've ever seen, and if anyone else has seen a cart bigger than this one, they've kept quiet about it! This is no horse-drawn cart. If my best team tried to shift it, their eyes would fall out!'

Toby and Bat heard about the cart and came to inspect it. Toby's forehead wrinkled up like a raisin when he saw the vehicle. He was so astonished, he forgot how miserable he felt.

'What do you say to this, then?' Dawkin asked him.

'If this ain't a proper poser,' rasped Toby, 'I'll be poleaxed, prodded and painted purple!'

Bat clambered up into the cart and found items of gigantic harness which he held up for Toby to look at.

'Did you ever see the like, Mr Hoken? What horse would wear a girth this size? I reckon this would fit round Nancy with no trouble at all!'

Some harness buckles caught the sun as Bat waved his arms about and the flash shone straight into Toby's eyes.

And with the flash came an idea so sudden and strong it felt like a slap on the back from a lightning bolt.

'Are you sure you're feeling quite all right?' Dawkin enquired. 'Your face has gone the colour of a cuttlefish consomme!'

'All right?' chortled Toby. 'All right?' He hugged Dawkin, then gave a hop and clicked

his heels together in mid-air. 'I'm in the pink! I'm delighted right down to the ends of my toenails! My teeth are a-tinglin'! Why, my corns are a-cuttin' capers! Don't you see? This 'ere cart is the answer!'

'Er, is that so?' said Dawkin, straightening his wig. 'Then what, pray, was the question?'

'Manure!' yelled Toby, rubbing his hands with glee.

'Where?' yelped Dawkin, casting a horrified glance at his breeches.

'No, no, you great lupin!' chuckled Toby. 'I mean elephant doin's! We get plenty of shovels and we load up this cart, then we 'arness Rita and Nancy to it and we drive it away!'

Toby folded his arms contentedly, his face a radiant red.

'Where?' asked Dawkin.

'Where what?'

Bat peeped over the side of the cart.

'Mr Dawkin means to ask where we're going to take the elephant muck,' he explained to Toby. 'We can drive it away from Feeblerick Hall all right, but what are we going to do with it after that?'

Toby spluttered like a saucepan boiling over and stamped his foot with frustration.

'I'll be rotated, roasted and rollicked!' he cursed. 'Some blessed 'itch always comes along to spoil things!' He sat down on the driveway, put his head in his hands and looked miserable again.

'I'm not sure I like this,' Dawkin informed Bat. 'Elephant carts don't generally appear out of nowhere! If I didn't know better, I'd say that magic was going on!'

Dawkin noticed the corners of the apprentice's mouth twitch. For a moment, he thought the lad was going to smile, but then Bat turned away and started clattering something in the back of the cart.

As amazed and dumbfounded as Dawkin and Toby Hoken were at the appearance of the cart, they would have been even more amazed and dumbfounded if, later that evening, they had overheard Bat in the elephant house. He was talking to Rita and Nancy and they gave every appearance of talking back, in a gruntly, snuffly, elephantine way.

'So!' Rita said excitedly. 'The cart came from you-know-what!'

'That's it,' replied Bat, 'and tomorrow we'll be off on a long journey.'

'What a lark!' squealed Rita.

'My dear,' Nancy told her, 'I'm a little older than you and more of an elephant-of-the-world. If you let yourself be guided by me and take my advice, I'm sure that we can get along with as few larks as possible.'

Rita ignored Nancy's suggestion and spoke to Bat again. 'What about Toby?' she asked. 'How does he feel about going you-know-where to meet you-know-who?'

'I haven't actually mentioned it yet,' Bat admitted. 'I've been waiting for the right time to tell him. I'm sure the right time and the right place will turn up as we're going along.'

'So considerate of others!' Nancy purred, patting Bat on the head with her trunk. 'Really, Rita, you could learn a thing or two from the way Bat behaves.'

'What, like walking on my hind legs?' chuckled Rita. 'Don't talk so daft!'

SIX

Turnip Scandal

Toby brooded all day and all night, but early the following morning he regained his good spirits. Rita and Nancy were harnessed to the cart which was pulled round to the pile of unmentionables at the back of the elephant house. Toby organised a team of workers from all over the estate, borrowed a bundle of shovels from the head gardener and supervised the loading of the cart.

'Now then, lads!' he told them. 'I don't want any of you to get shy and start a-ticklin' it! There's plenty for everybody, so get stuck in!'

The team worked hard and the cart was fully loaded by late afternoon.

'Well, Bat,' said Toby as the last shoveller shuffled off, bent-backed, 'that's a good job done and no mistake!'

'But what now, Mr Hoken?'

'Never you mind!' Toby chuckled, tapping a finger against the side of his nose. 'As my old grandad used to say – when the cuckoo comes to the bare thorn, sell your cow and buy your corn!'

'What does that mean, Mr Hoken?'

'Danged if I know!' admitted Toby. 'I 'ardly understood a word my old grandad said! Still, mount up, lad! Let's get this manure on the move!'

The twisty lane behind the elephant house joined a wide road like a brook flowing into a river. The afternoon sun poured down between the branches of the trees, casting shadows over the flanks of the elephants.

'Look at those flowers over there!' Rita kept exclaiming. 'Look at those trees!'

'Don't trumpet so, dear!' Nancy advised. 'It's all right for an elephant to be interested in edible plants, but knowing the names of too many wild flowers smacks of swank!'

'Er . . . Mr Hoken,' said Bat, 'doesn't this road go through Chewlow?'

'Aye!'

'Do you think it's a good idea to drive the cart down the main street?'

'Course it is!' Toby replied irritably. 'We're takin' our muck to the village dump and this is the quickest way.'

'But – '

'But nothin'!' snapped Toby. 'I'm the master, you're the 'prentice, remember? If you've got any better ideas, lad, let's be 'earin' 'em!'

'I thought we might . . .' Bat's voice died to a whisper as he saw the look on Toby's face. The wind sighed through the trees as though it were whispering back.

Meanwhile, on the village green in Chewlow, an important event was in full swing. Chewlow was battling it out with the village of Wickworthy in the finals of the County Turnip-hurling Championship. A large crowd had assembled to watch and the parish councils of both villages were seated on a raised platform to have a good view of the epic struggle. There were lots of 'oohs!' and 'aahs!' from the crowd. Gradually, however, the attention of the spectators was diverted from the match.

It began with the faintest tang of elephant unmentionables in the air. The Chewlovians, accustomed to the smell, didn't flinch, but the Wickworthians twitched their noses and eyed their neighbours suspiciously. The tang grew to a whiff which quickly swelled into a

stench. Cats spat, hissed and ran. Dogs went round in whining circles with their tails between their legs. The Wickworthy Turnip-hurling team went cross-eyed and turnips went flying all over the place.

Samson Thirkettle, chairman of the Wickworthy parish council, leapt to his feet and pointed an accusing finger at Councillor Earwacker's chubby chest.

'There's something fishy going on round here!' he choked. 'I suspect foul play! Well, something around here smells foul, anyway. It's my opinion that your team is using unfair tactics to win the championship! In fact, I think the whole village is cheating!'

'Cheating?' spluttered Councillor Earwacker. 'Why, I've never been so insulted in my life!'

'You surprise me!' coughed Samson Thirkettle. 'Come, councillors! Let's return to Wickworthy with all possible haste! I intend to write a strongly worded letter to the County Sheriff on the subject of the cheats of Chewlow!'

By the time the elephant cart rumbled into sight, the road into Chewlow was blocked by an angry crowd waving pitchforks, cudgels and turnips. At the head of the crowd stood

Councillor Earwacker, puffed up with rage and self-importance. He had twined sprigs of lavender and cloves into his moustache to counteract the stink from the cart. His hand was held up in a sign of restraint. His fat fingers looked like a bunch of pink gherkins.

'Halt!' he cried. 'Just what do you mean by bringing that heap of festering filth into our village?'

'I don't mean anythin'!' said Toby. 'I just want to unload this cart on the dump at the end of Martin's Lane.'

The crowd grumbled at Toby like an empty stomach.

'Who's the angry man with the wibbly-wobbly chins?' whispered Rita.

'A person of no breeding and few manners,' said Nancy. 'Just ignore him, dear!'

'You shallow-brained, addle-pated noodle!' raged Councillor Earwacker. 'It states quite clearly in the local by-laws that the Martin's Lane dump is only for household rubbish or waste from any factory licensed according to Council By-law Thirty-two! You can't put any old garbage on our rubbish dump!'

'But this is 'ouse'old rubbish!' Toby protested. 'Elephant 'ouse'old rubbish!'

Someone in the crowd threw a turnip straight at Toby's head. Rita raised her trunk casually, caught the turnip and popped it into her mouth, where she crushed it contentedly.

'Ta, everso, I'm sure!' she murmured.

'If you don't turn round and get out of here,' Councillor Earwacker threatened, 'I shall send for a beadle to have you detained!'

The crowd growled its approval and brandished its turnips. Toby's temper began to rise. 'Why, you jumped-up jackanapes!' he muttered. 'I'll be dished, drilled and devilled if I don't – '

'Mr Hoken!' whispered Bat. 'Let's do as they say! They might hurt the elephants!'

Toby looked at the faces of the villagers and saw that Bat was right.

'Come, Rita, Nancy!' he said scornfully. 'This place ain't fit for the likes of us!' He pulled gently on the reins and the elephants slowly turned, pulling the cart away from Chewlow.

Councillor Earwacker dusted his hands and adjusted his cravat. 'The sooner those pesky elephants are tinned, the better!' he said, but he waited until Toby Hoken was out of earshot before he said it.

SEVEN

Morton Tops

As the cart trundled away from Chewlow, Toby grumbled to himself.

'I dunno! Plagued and persecuted by pettifoggers, that's what I am! And I'm 'ungry! No lunch, no tea! I'm that starvin', if you put that Earwacker chap between two slices of bread, I'd eat 'im – waistcoat, bowler 'at and all!'

Bat gave a smile that curled across his face as snugly as a sleeping dormouse. 'Why don't we stop along the road for a spot of something, Mr Hoken?' he suggested.

'Like what, lad?'

'I brought a few things along with me, just in case,' Bat replied. 'A few apples, some cheese, a loaf, a cold chicken, a jug of milk, a flagon of cider – '

Toby shot his apprentice a sharp glance. 'Anyone'd think you knew we were goin' to

47

get turfed out of the village!'

Bat shrugged. 'It never does any harm to be prepared.'

They pulled off the road and Bat brought a wicker basket out from under the driver's seat. There was even a small sack of apples for the elephants. They were the last apples from the winter store – a bit wrinkled, but as sweet as summer.

As Toby ate, he kept a wary eye on the darkening sky and lengthening shadows. 'Best to get back before nightfall!' he observed.

'Well, to tell you the truth, Mr Hoken, I've had a bit of an idea about the elephant problem. If we set off now and travelled through the night . . . !'

'Travel through the night!' mocked Toby. 'Don't talk daft, lad! Without lanterns we'd be as blind as moles!'

'Oh, I brought some lanterns!' Bat announced cheerfully. 'I thought it might be a good idea to pack a couple just in case! Shall I light them, Mr Hoken? Er . . . Mr Hoken?'

Toby's face looked as far-off as the moon through a thin cloud. 'Blind as moles, eh?' he said to himself. 'Well, I'll be chased, chafed and chivvied if that ain't the very thing!' He threw a slice of bread into the air. Nancy caught it smartly with her trunk and popped it into her mouth with a happy grunt.

'Moles!' Toby exclaimed, slapping his thigh. 'That's it, Bat! We'll bung this load of muck underground! We'll bury it deeper than the meanest pirate ever buried a treasure chest!'

'But how – '

'Soon as it's dark, we'll slip up to the old silver mine at Morton Tops,' said Toby. 'It's been years since it's been worked! They do say the old shaft is so deep that if you drop a ripe tomato down it on Friday night, you won't 'ear it squelch till Monday mornin'!'

'But, Mr Hoken,' said Bat, 'don't you think it might be a better idea if we – '

'Listen, lad,' said Toby, wagging his finger. 'I'm an old bird, wise in the ways of the world and you're no more'n a fluffy chick! If I say the mine shaft at Morton Tops, then that's it and no more about it!'

'Yes, Mr Hoken,' sighed Bat. 'I was just wondering . . . well, what if the mine is still being used?'

'The last silver was taken out of that mine when my dad was a-courtin' my old ma! You light those lanterns and let's get ready. We don't want 'igh-and-mighty Earwacker to catch us at it! Bound to be against some blessed rule or another!'

The first stars were glimmering when they set off. Toby drove the cart up Silver Lane, which wound its way up the side of Beacon Hill and led out on to the windswept plain of Morton Tops. They followed old miners' trails that were almost overgrown with bracken until they reached the battered wooden fence that surrounded the mine shaft. By the light of the lanterns, they were just able to make out the faded lettering on a sign:

PRIVATE PROPERTY
KEEP OUT!
TRESPASSERS WILL BE PEELED!

'Oh dear!' groaned Bat, biting his bottom lip. 'Suppose the owner catches us?'

'Stop your grizzlin', lad!' said Toby. 'The owner of this mine 'as been pushin' up daisies for forty years or more! Jump down and give us an 'and with this 'ere fence!'

With the help of the elephants, it was the work of a few moments to open a wide gap in the fence. Rita and Nancy pulled up old palings and cast them aside as eagerly as

small children unwrapping presents. A few scrubby metres away the mine shaft yawned like a circle made of night.

'This is it!' bubbled Toby. 'In an hour or two, our troubles will be over! Mr Waldo Faldo will 'ave to look elsewhere for 'is precious profit! And the beauty of it is, we ain't causin' no nuisance to anyone!'

'That's what he thinks!' Bat whispered to the elephants.

'Are you going to tell him about you-know-who?' asked Rita.

'I don't think this is the right time or place,' said Bat, 'but I'm going to use a little you-know-what!'

So saying, Bat reached inside his shirt, clutched tightly at something hanging round his neck and mouthed silent words.

'Come on, lad!' chirped Toby. 'Let's drop the back of the cart and start shovellin'!'

Under cover of the dark, Bat continued his soundless talk. Toby was too busy and too pleased to notice.

When all was ready, the old keeper raised a hefty shovelful of elephant unmentionables and paused for a moment. 'I'd like to dedicate this first shovel of muck to Councillor Earwacker!' he said grandly, then he swung his arms and the muck slid off the shovel into the blackness of the shaft.

'Oi!' squealed angry, echoey voices. 'What's the big idea? What's goin' on?'

Toby stared at Bat in disbelief. The voices had come from out of the mine shaft – and it did not stop at the voices. Lights appeared at the mouth of the old mine and floated towards the elephant cart.

EIGHT

Clods

The lights were candles, flickering on the brims of hats worn by tiny men and women, walking in single file. The men had bushy beards that came down to their chests, the women had black, glossy hair. Both men and women wore dusty overalls and carried miniature picks and shovels.

Leading the line was an angry-looking woman whose hat and overalls were heavily splattered with elephant unmentionables. She walked straight into the pool of light from Toby's lantern, stuck her pick into the ground, folded her arms and glared at the old elephant keeper.

'Was it you who just chucked a shovelful of elephant nasty into our mine?' she demanded in a voice as sparky as two flints being knocked together.

'And what if it was?' replied Toby defiantly.

The tiny woman's eyes flashed like frosty granite. 'If it was you, Grandad, I'd warn you not to do it again! Because if you do, I'll swarm up your coat and punch you right on the nose!'

The tiny men and women clapped and cheered when they heard this. One or two put their fingers in their mouths and whistled piercingly.

Toby waited until the rumpus had died down and said, with an uncertain jeer in his voice, 'You gotta mighty mouth for one so

small, ain't you? 'Oo d'you reckon you are, any road?'

The tiny people gasped and tutted, but the woman in the lantern light simply blinked. 'I'm Clara Chubnutt, Grandad!' she said haughtily. 'And I'm guardian of this mine! It's ours now, and has been ever since the Clods finished with it!'

There was more clapping and whistling.

'And 'oo are the Clods?' Toby demanded.

'You are!' Clara informed him. 'A great, ham-fisted, loud-voiced, clumping-footed Clod of a human being!'

'Oh, and you're not 'uman, I suppose?' Toby snapped sarcastically.

The silence that followed this remark was so icy it would have frozen a penguin's bottom solid.

Clara drew herself up to the top of her one-metre-point-nothing and bellowed, 'Human? Human? I wouldn't be anything so common! I'm a dwarf! We're all dwarfs and proud of it! You Clods come along and rip up the poor old Earth without so much as a by-your-leave! You take what you want, make a complete mess of everything and then just saunter away feeling oh-so-smug and pleased with yourselves! That's when the dwarfs step in to try and put things back to rights – and hard work it is too!' Clara pointed a blunt finger at Toby. 'And we can do without you coming along and throwing elephant nasty all over us, thank you very much! You Clods have made enough mess around here already! Be off with you!'

There were indignant growls and mocking whoops from the other dwarfs.

'Mr Hoken?' said Bat softly. 'I don't think this is a good place to dump the load. I think it would be better to back off and leave this place to them!'

Toby sighed deeply and nodded, but didn't say a word. He put the back of the cart up, hauled himself up into the driver's seat and urged the elephants into a lumber. In the dark behind them, the dwarfs filed back to their work.

After a long time, Toby said, 'I think that what just 'appened better stay a secret between the two of us, lad.'

'Why's that, then, Mr Hoken?'

'See, Bat, there's things people believe no matter 'ow stupid they seem, and then there's things people won't ever believe, no matter 'ow sensible. Elephant muck now, people find that easy to believe. But dwarfs . . . ' Toby clicked his tongue and shook his head. 'Dwarfs is somethin' else!'

'Mr Hoken,' said Bat, 'don't you think the best thing would be to – '

'Don't chatter on so!' grumbled Toby. 'I'm ponderin'. This is a big load of manure and it'll take a deep think to see things straight!'

Toby was so rapt in thought he didn't notice Bat turn to the night, hold up his hands and say, 'What can I do?' If he had, he would have thought it odd, since Bat appeared to be addressing the black, empty air.

It was late when they arrived back at the Hall. Once Rita and Nancy were safe back in their stalls, Bat climbed up to his bed in the hay loft.

'Is there going to be much more of this gallivanting around?' Nancy asked him. 'I find all the excitement rather exhausting!'

'You heard Toby talking about the dwarfs,' said Rita. 'If he feels like that about something he's seen with his own eyes, what do you think he'd do if Bat told him about you-know-what? Toby needs careful handling!'

'Toby,' sighed Nancy, 'needs his head replacing with a coconut!'

Meanwhile, in his little cottage, Toby lay on his bed. Tired as he was, the old man found sleep harder to come by than an Easter egg on Christmas Eve. He lay awake, brooding. Faces and voices rattled around in his brain like coffee beans in a grinder.

'Can't chuck it in Chewlow!' he groaned. 'Can't shove it down a shaft! I'll be cracked, canned and chromed if I know what to do with it! It needs a good, long, deep think and no mistake!'

NINE

Foulmire Forest

Bat was an early riser, but when he woke the following morning, he found old Toby up before him. When the apprentice poked his tousled head out from the hay loft, he saw Toby bustling about as busily as a bluebottle in a jam factory.

'Morning, Mr Hoken!' Bat yawned.

'Mornin'?' laughed Toby. 'Why, the best part of the day's already over, lad! I've already mucked the elephants out, fed and watered 'em and they're 'arnessed up ready to go! My old grandad used to say that the worm 'oo gets up afore the early bird never gets caught!'

Bat scratched his head and blinked against the light. 'I've had a great idea about the elephants!' he said. 'Why don't we – '

'And I've 'ad an even better idea!' Toby butted in. 'I'm gonna show 'em, lad! The bird ain't been born that gets up early enough to catch old Toby Hoken out, oh no!' He grinned up at Bat. There were so many gaps in Toby's grin that it was like being smiled at by a piano. 'Come on, lad!' the old man urged. 'We got a tidy way to go, and time's a-wastin'!' They set off in bright sunshine. Clouds moved across the sky like a procession of white elephants.

'Where are we off to, Mr Hoken?' asked Bat.

'Let that be a surprise!' Toby replied mysteriously. 'But I can tell you one thing, our road lies through Foulmire Forest!'

Bat shuddered. No one went near Foulmire Forest unless they had to. There were strange sounds and peculiar lights in the forest at night. Folk told tales about the place that made hedgehogs curl up and horses bolt. It was said that the animals in the forest were so savage that if they didn't bite, claw or sting, then they swallowed whole. Except for the trees, the plants that grew there were poisonous and anyone who drank from Foulmire's streams or springs would be covered in warts from head to toe.

'Don't you worry, lad!' Toby assured Bat. 'We'll be travellin' in broad daylight. Besides, you don't wanna go believin' all those tales people tell about Foulmire. Only 'alf of 'em are true!'

Foulmire Forest was gloomy. Its shadows sucked the warmth from the sun so that the light filtering down through the trees looked pale and poorly as an overstuffed glutton. Rita and Nancy didn't like the place. They snuffled and whuffed and twined trunks for comfort. Toby sang and whistled and tried to sound carefree, but his eyes flicked from side to side as anxiously as a snake-charmer with a loose cobra.

No birds sang, no rabbits bobbed across the road, no deer watched from the undergrowth. Some of the trees were swathed in moss-covered vines and every stump and fallen trunk bristled with gaudy toadstools.

At length the road led to a wide stone bridge that crossed a slow-moving stream.

'Er, Mr Hoken,' Bat said nervously, 'I've never been here before, of course, but I've got a funny sort of feeling that it's not a good idea to cross here. If we turn right and go on for about ten minutes, we might find a ford!'

'What are you babblin' about, Bat?' Toby asked. 'What's the point in goin' out of our

way when there's a sturdy stone bridge straight ahead?'

'It looks spooky!' said Bat.

'Don't talk such poppycock!' scoffed Toby. "Ooever 'eard of a spooky bridge?'

At that moment there was a wild cry, a flash of blue lightning and a figure appeared in the middle of the bridge.

The elephants flapped their ears and trumpeted. Toby's face went paler than a peeled boiled egg and Bat rolled his eyes despairingly.

The creature barring their way was tall and scrawny. It had a face like a grey goldfish, teeth like neglected tombstones and eyes like yellow marbles. Its clothes were made of canvas. The hand it held out had nails like black almonds.

'Halt!' the creature screeched. 'If you value your lives!'

Toby halted the cart and tried to act as calmly as possible, but the reins trembled in his hands.

"Oo are you?' he asked. 'What d'you want?'

The creature's grey lips twisted into a mirthless smile. 'I am Hengist the Hobgoblin!' it declared. 'And I want all your gold! If you don't give me gold, I shall say one of my wicked spells and turn you into a stoat!'

'We 'aven't got any gold!' said Toby.

'Your silver, then!' cried Hengist. 'Your shining, newly-minted coins, your bright bracelets, give them all to me, or it's stoat, stoat, stoat for you!'

'Ain't got no silver, neither!' said Toby.

'What?' shouted Hengist peevishly. 'How about copper, then? Any lead? Zinc?'

'Nope!' said Toby.

'Well, what have you got?' snapped the hobgoblin.

'Elephant unmentionables,' said Toby. 'A 'uge great cartful of steamin' elephants' doin's!'

'Yee-ukk!' squealed Hengist. 'That is *so* sick! I'm going to say my wicked spell and turn you into a stoat for being so weird!' The hobgoblin waved its hands, opened its mouth and then, all of a sudden, nothing happened. Hengist stood as stiff and still as a meringue.

'What's a-goin' on?' whispered Toby.

Bat hurriedly took his hand out of his shirt and coughed. 'Oh, er, nothing, Mr Hoken! I think the hobgoblin's magic must have gone a bit wrong! Let's get Nancy to pick it up and pitch it into the water, shall we?'

'Well really!' Nancy complained as she wrapped her trunk around Hengist's waist. 'I'm just glad my family can't see me now! They would never have dreamed that I'd ever get mixed up with petrified hobgoblins! If you ask me, Bat, the sooner you tell Toby Hoken about you-know-who, the better!'

Toby watched sourly as Hengist splashed into the stream and floated out of sight.

'Dwarfs!' he said to himself. "Obgoblins! I'll be filleted, fried and fricasseed if there ain't somethin' peculiar a-goin' on!'

TEN

A Marine Monarch

Despite Toby's misgivings, nothing else peculiar happened that morning. In fact, the remainder of the journey through Foulmire Forest was so uneventful that the old elephant keeper fell into a doze as soft as a gerbil's chest. When he woke, he found the cart was out on the open road passing across a dark heath. He also found his apprentice was staring at him suspiciously.

'I can smell salt, Mr Hoken, and when the wind sits in the south-west, I can hear a sighing sound like waves breaking in the distance. Are we headed for the sea?'

'We are!' Toby affirmed.

Bat glanced behind him at the load and his eyes widened in shock. 'But you don't mean – you're not thinking of – '

'If I should take a fancy to a day at the seaside, where's the 'arm in it?' Toby said with a wink. 'And if I 'appen to arrive at the seaside with a full elephant cart and leave with an empty 'un, 'oo's to notice? I said it needed a good deep think, and I've come up with a good, deep answer. Ain't nothin' deeper than the sea, I reckon. There's more than enough water in it to wash away all our elephant unmentionables and nobody need be any the wiser!'

'But we can't!' protested Bat. 'What about the fish?'

'I've always 'eard tell as 'ow there's plenty of fish in the sea,' said Toby stubbornly. 'I can't see that a few less would make much difference! But what I can see is that the week's more than 'alf over and we're no nearer gettin' rid of this muck than we were at the start of it! I can feel Waldo Faldo's scented breath on the back of my neck, an' it gives me the collywobbles!'

'But, Mr Hoken!' cried Bat. 'What we ought to have done all along is – '

'Look there!' shouted Toby.

Directly ahead, the road sloped down. At the bottom of the slope the sea blazed in the afternoon sunlight as it burst over dark rocks and creamed itself to foam along a beach of pale sand. Rita raised her trunk and roared excitedly.

'Ooh, I do love the seaside! D'you think I'll find a "kiss me quick" hat big enough to wear?'

'Rita, *really*!' sighed Nancy.

'No towns, no villages, not even a fisherman's cottage!' said Toby. 'There ain't a more deserted spot for miles! No spyin' eyes to see us, no waggin' tongues to tell us we're goin' against regulations! 'Tis perfect, lad!'

Bat said nothing, but he slipped his hand into his shirt and closed his fingers on something hanging round his neck.

Toby turned the cart on to a track that twisted off the main road and wound like a wounded worm down to a broad, flat shelf of rock. At the edge of the rock was a short drop into heaving water that made a sound slurpier than a chef tasting soup.

'Just the spot!' beamed Toby as he parked the cart on the brink of the drop. 'We'll 'ave a bite to eat and then we'll get down to some serious shovellin'!'

Toby ate with a light heart, which grew even lighter after several long pulls from a stone ale jug. Nancy and Rita were loosed from their harness and, after feeding, discovered some shallow pools. Even Nancy could not resist filling up her trunk with sea water and playing squirting games.

Only Bat did not seem to be enjoying himself. He picked at the food and kept casting anxious glances over his shoulder.

'What's up, Bat?' asked Toby. 'You're jumpier than a flea on a farrier's forearm! There's no use in lookin' be'ind you all the time, lad! There's nothin' to see but the sea!'

The ale made this comment into one of the wittiest jokes Toby had ever heard and he laughed heartily at it. Still laughing, he dropped the tail of the cart, climbed into the back and playfully hefted a shovelful of muck.

'Ha-one!' he chucked. 'Ha-two! H-a-a-a-a!' The cry of alarm turned into a cry of pain as Toby dropped the shovel on to his foot.

Two green eyes glowered up out of the water. The jerking waves suddenly reared up to form the head and shoulders of an enormous man. His long hair and beetling eyebrows were formed by white wave-tops. He had a straggling seaweed beard and shell teeth. Screaming gulls circled round his head as he bent his white brows into an angry frown and opened his mouth to speak. Toby winced, expecting to be blasted by a roar like

a spring tide. Instead, the sea-giant's voice was as gentle as the toes of a toddler dabbling in the shallows.

'I say, you there! Chappie with the shovel! What are you playing at?'

Toby shook his head to try and clear the ale fumes away.

'Bat?' he croaked. 'Can you see what I see?'

'I can, Mr Hoken.'

'I was afraid of that!' Toby groaned.

The giant leaned closer and sniffed at the cart. 'What a corking pong!' he exclaimed. 'A dab or two of that behind one's ears and even a starving giant squid would leave one well alone! Now then, you old scoundrel, perhaps you can explain yourself.'

'Well, your honour,' quailed Toby. 'I was just goin' to sprinkle a bit of this 'ere elephant dung into the sea, like.'

'Into the sea?' the giant repeated angrily. 'You mean you were going to pitch this pile of pachyderm poop into the emerald waters of one's peaceful domain? You cheeky old chap! One's got a good mind to nip up an estuary and flood your privy! Where did you get the right to throw rubbish in the sea?'

'Well, your honour,' blushed Toby, 'I didn't think anyone would mind, like.'

'Well, one does mind!' said the giant. 'And if you fling so much as a single lump of elephant's thingy into one's pellucid waves, one will be forced to cut up rough and give you a glimpse of Davy Jones' locker!'

'So sorry, your honour!' Toby said shamedly. 'I won't do it again, I'm sure!'

And with the giant's indignant eyes staring on, the elephants were harnessed up and the cart set off back to the main road.

'Was that great big chap in the water you-know-who, Nancy?' Rita asked.

'Certainly not! That was an aristocrat!' Nancy replied. 'An incredibly large aristocrat. They get that way at times – it's all the banqueting, you know. Aristocrats often bathe in the sea for their health.'

'Don't they do it for fun?' puzzled Rita.

'No,' Nancy told her. 'Aristocrats are far too busy leading a life of leisure to have fun!'

Up in the driving seat, meanwhile, Toby was despairing. 'That's it!' he grizzled. 'Rita and Nancy are as good as tom-cat tuck already! Soon as I get an idea up pop councillors, dwarfs, 'obgoblins and marine monarchs! Everythin's agin me!' Toby opened his mouth to wail and, much to his surprise, Bat clipped a slab of chewy toffee into it. Toby's jaws locked at once.

'I'm sorry, Mr Hoken,' Bat apologised, 'but it's the only way I could think of getting you to keep quiet. If you'd listened to me in the first place, we could have saved a lot of time. We need to take some advice about this elephant muck and the best advice we can get is from the Wise Man of Malarkey Mountain. I say we take the next road north and go to him!'

'Well, hurray!' cheered Rita. 'Bat's told Toby about you-know-who at last!'

ELEVEN

To Malarkey Mountain

When Toby heard Bat mention the wise man, his eyes bulged out with alarm. Anything to do with magic made him feel nervous, and the Wise Man of Malarkey Mountain was said to be so magic that even stories about him set Toby's toes trembling in his boots. Some said the wise man lived alone on top of a mountain because he had once spoken too frankly to a short-tempered tyrant in a far-off land and was now hiding from assassins. Some said he was a great wizard, thousands of years old who kept himself to himself for fear that someone would steal the secret of eternal life from him. Others said he was an old lunatic who lived in solitude because he was battier than a cathedral bell-tower.

It took Toby a good while to chew his way out of the toffee and his jaw muscles ached so much afterwards that he was unable to talk for an hour. What he was able to do was think.

'You could be right, Bat,' he admitted at last. 'But it's a desperate business! I'll be scuttled, skinned and scoured if the thought of gettin' mixed up with magic don't make my blood run chillier than a frozen ferret!' Toby shivered, then sighed. 'Pity we ain't got time to nip back to the 'all to pick up some creature comforts for the journey. But there we are, needs must when the devil drives!'

'Oh, not to worry!' Bat said airily. 'I brought a few extra things along in case they came in handy!'

'What things?' enquired Toby.

'Enough food for a couple of days, some pillows and blankets, a groundsheet, a change of clothes, a tinder-box, a cooking pot, some cutlery, soap and towels – oh, and some hay and cabbages for the elephants, of course! I just grabbed a few things that came to hand.'

'Young whippersnapper you may be,' rasped Toby, 'but there's times I suspect you know a lot more than you let on, lad!'

Toby, Bat and the elephants fed well and slept comfortably that night. Early next morning they were woken by the song of a blackbird and after breakfast they set off on the Great North Road.

It was not a pleasant journey. The warm weather ripened up the smell of the elephant unmentionables and the wind wafted the scent ahead. It made cows lie down in the fields and caused sheep to stampede. When the cart passed through villages, doors were slammed angrily and people with wooden pegs on their noses leaned out of windows to shake their fists and shout abuse.

Toby and Bat, who had long grown used to the aroma, sat grim-mouthed and silent on the driver's seat.

Just before noon, they had their first sight of Malarkey Mountain. It was shaped like a giant's shoulder and the sprinkling of snow near the summit looked like flakes of dandruff. The flanks of the mountain were green with fir trees. Ravens cawed from the tops of the trees, or flapped across the sky as clumsy as flying vicars.

By late afternoon they reached the foot of the mountain where they paused to read a large sign.

'MALARKEY MOUNTAIN,' it read, 'HEIGHT: Plenty! POPULATION: One wise man plus toads, lizards, snakes, goats, rabbits – the place is hopping with them. Wolves too, maybe – who knows? Also there are creepy-crawlies so big, if you saw them your face would go the colour of chicken soup, I'm telling you. Who needs a wise man anyway? You need to make your mind up about something? Go home, talk it over with a friend, toss a coin! Do yourself a favour, turn back!'

Beyond the sign, a narrow track zigzagged upwards.

'We'll never get the cart up there!' Toby observed.

'That won't be a problem!' said Bat briskly. He hopped down from the cart and whispered to Rita and Nancy as he unharnessed them.

'What do you say, ladies?'

'We're old enough to take care of ourselves, my dear!' Rita announced gamely. 'You leave us here and take old Toby up the mountain.'

'I agree,' said Nancy. 'We shall be perfectly all right. If anyone accosts us, we shall squash them. We don't mind being left on our own half as much as we'd mind being eaten out of tins by cats!'

'I dunno!' complained Toby as he climbed out of the cart with a face as long as a wet Wednesday. 'Bossed about by an apprentice and two elephants! And at my time of life, too!'

'Come on, Mr Hoken!' grinned Bat. 'Best foot forward! Like your old grandad used to say, first hand to the spoon gets the skin off the custard!'

'Ah!' Toby nodded sagely, then his face sank like a ruined soufflé. ''Ere! 'Ow did you know my old grandad used to say that?'

'Lucky guess!' said Bat.

After they had gone a few metres along the path, Toby looked behind and saw that there was writing on the back of the sign.

'It's your decision,' it said, 'but don't say I didn't warn you!'

'I'll be picked, pipped and puréed before today's out!' Toby muttered. 'You mark my words!'

TWELVE

On the Track

Toby wasn't picked, pipped or puréed, but he hadn't gone far along the mountain track before he was pelted. A band of stormy cloud swept across the sky and threw down a shower of cold rain that draggled Toby's hair and sent drips down the back of his neck.

'Man of my age ought to be wrapped up cozy in a rockin' chair,' he wheezed, 'not cavortin' about in soggy britches on a mountainside! Wouldn't surprise me if I caught a cold, now, on top of everythin' else! Most likely it'll go down on to my chest and turn to pneumonia!' He sighed deeply. 'If I didn't 'ave a naturally cheerful nature, there's times I'd be tempted to look on the black side!'

The way grew steeper and more slippery and soon Toby had no breath to spare for complaining. A low cloud rolled in and hugged Malarkey Mountain like a grey bear, so that Bat and Toby could see no further than a few metres. An hour after the mist came, the track forked and the travellers paused, uncertain.

'Well, lad?' panted Toby. 'What do we do now?'

'We ask someone the way,' said Bat.

'A brilliant plan, lad,' Toby said sarcastically, 'the only drawback bein' there ain't a blessed soul *to* ask! Unless, of course . . .'

While Toby chuntered on, Bat put his hand into his shirt and whispered.

'I suppose I could always do this – ' said Toby, holding out his arm, ' – and then do this – ' he snapped his fingers ' – and 'ope someone we could ask would just appear out of nowhere!'

And a huge owl swept silently out of the mist and alighted on Toby's outstretched arm. The grip of its talons made Toby gulp like a disappointed frog. The owl turned its golden eyes on the old man and began a trilling hoot that went on for some time.

'It was me who sent for you, actually,' Bat told the owl. 'I'm sorry to drag you out in weather like this, but we don't know our way.'

The owl hooted with irritation, clucked, opened its wings and soared off.

'We take the right fork!' Bat said confidently.

Toby frowned at his apprentice. 'Where did you learn owl-callin', lad?' he asked. 'And 'oo taught you 'ow to speak Owl?'

'Can't really remember,' said Bat. 'I must have sort of picked them up as I went along.'

"Ow the 'ell d'you sort of pick up talkin' to owls?' Toby asked heatedly, but Bat had already walked on and seemed not to hear the question.

At dusk, the track rose out of the mist and they could see the first stars of evening quivering.

'We can't go much further, lad!' said Toby. 'It'll be night soon. We can't see our way in the dark!'

'We can't,' agreed Bat. 'But he can.'

Toby turned and jumped nervously as he saw a big wild-cat crouching beside the path. The cat's eyes burned green and its tufted ears were as pointed as a devil's horns. When it saw Toby the beast fluffed up its fur and gave a growling purr that sounded like a sewing machine losing its temper.

'This is your doin', I suppose?' Toby

demanded hoarsely.

'Er, I'm afraid so, Mr Hoken.'

'Summat else you just sort of picked up as you went along?'

'The cat will be happy to lead us to the wise man,' said Bat, avoiding the question.

The cat bared its teeth and hissed louder than a red-hot horseshoe being dipped in a water trough.

'If that animal's 'appy,' Toby mused, 'I wouldn't like to meet it when it was aggravated!'

They followed the cat through the deepening dark while the cold stiffened their wet clothes and ached in their joints. A copper-coloured moon began to rise over the shoulder of the mountain.

'If we walk much further,' said Toby, 'we'll be able to shake 'ands with the man in the moon, and give 'is dog a pat on the 'ead!'

But even as he groused, he caught sight of a distant light. It was a candle, gleaming in the window of a log cabin.

'I'll tell you what, Bat,' Toby admitted. 'I've never met a wise man before and the thought of it makes me more nervous than a jelly at a birthday party! What if 'e ain't pleased to see us? I'd 'ate to come all this way just to be 'arried, 'exed and 'ornswaggled!'

Bat had no time to reply, for as they approached, the door of the cabin swung open and the Wise Man of Malarkey Mountain stepped out.

THIRTEEN

Roses and Rhubarb

If the wise man had worn a pointed hat and a white beard reaching down to his ankles, Toby wouldn't have been surprised. If the wise man had carried a vulture on his shoulder and hurled a thunderbolt to transform him into an earwig, it would have been no more than Toby expected. As it turned out, the old elephant keeper was totally gob-smacked.

The Wise Man of Malarkey Mountain was chunky and chubby with rosy cheeks, a smile as wide as a slice of melon and eyes as shiny as a pat of fresh butter. He wore corded velvet trousers, a thick woollen jumper and soft leather mountain boots.

'Welcome, welcome!' he called. His voice was as comforting as a bubbling saucepan. 'Come in before you perish with the cold!'

He ushered the weary travellers into the

cabin and before he shut the door, he said something to the wild-cat that made it frisk its tail and bound away down the track.

Inside the cabin, a coal fire beamed in a black iron hearth. Candlelight glistened on polished wood and copper pans. A cuckoo clock ticked loudly on one wall. There was a trestle-table on which stood two steaming bowls. The whole cabin was filled with a delicious fragrance.

'I made you some bean soup,' said the wise man. 'Sit down! Eat! Enjoy!'

There was nutty brown bread to go with the soup and good, strong cheese to follow. And when the meal was finished and the table had been cleared, the wise man poured three tiny glasses of a cordial that winked like starlight, tasted like raspberries and left Toby and Bat's insides as warm as cough-drops.

The wise man set down his glass and said, 'So, Toby Hoken, you have a problem.'

"Ow come you know my name?' Toby glowered.

'I'm a wise man,' said the wise man holding up his palms.

'Well,' Toby said huffily, 'if you're so all-fired wise, you should know what my problem is without my 'avin' to say anythin'!'

The wise man grinned ruefully. 'I can't deny you're right. I know all about your little elephant problem – well, maybe not so little. But if I'd mentioned it right away, you might have thought I was some kind of show-off. I've been expecting you for days – so what took you so long?'

'I'll tell you what took so long,' Toby declared. 'My young apprentice and myself 'ave been through the most frantic frenzied and fantastical adventures, the like of which you've never heard before!'

'So tell me about it,' said the wise man.

And Toby did. He launched into a description of the problems at Feeblerick Hall and the journey they had caused that was as long and detailed as only he knew how to make it. The wise man was a good listener. He raised his eyebrows, put his hand to his mouth and exclaimed, 'You don't say!' in all the right places.

When Toby finished, the wise man sat back in his chair with one hand on his ample stomach. He waved his other hand through the air as though he were reeling cotton in on his fingers.

'So . . .' he mused, 'here's a big cart filled with what elephants have to do and it's causing a big fuss and bother! Here's a fat parish councillor in love with how important he is, and here's an oily businessman in love with his wallet! And over here, we have two gentle, affectionate elephants who are going to go on making more problems . . .'

'Aye!' Toby nodded. 'And if we can't put the stuff on a dump, or drop it down a mine shaft, or shovel it into the sea, what the blue blazes *are* we gonna do with it?'

'Well, Toby Hoken,' the wise man said slowly, 'I suggest you get people to put it on their rhubarb and their roses.'

Toby was convinced the wise man was mad. 'People are never gonna put elephant muck on rhubarb!' he exclaimed. 'They're too fond of custard! and 'oo's gonna want to smell roses if they got dung all over 'em?'

'Toby, Toby!' the wise man said patiently. 'I meant, put elephant droppings on the rhubarb while it's still growing. Spread it round the roots of rose trees. You've seen what horse manure does for roses, think what elephant manure would do! Roses the size of cauliflowers with thorns like tusks and what a perfume! Sticks of rhubarb as thick as trunks – think of the pies and crumbles and syllabubs!'

The wise man made magic with his words – Toby tasted the sharp fruitiness of the elephant rhubarb and his nose was filled with the velvety-sweet scent of elephant roses. Without knowing anything about it, Toby fell sound asleep.

The wise man looked across the table at Bat and smiled. 'You've done well, Bartholomew,' he said. 'You used your magic gently. That's good.'

'It took me a long time to conjure up the cart!' Bat complained. 'I still don't see why I couldn't use magic to make the manure vanish right at the start!'

'Too flashy!' chuckled the wise man. 'You use your magic too openly and people start getting frightened of you. For magic to be useful, you have to be subtle. Use it to persuade people into doing the right thing. Show me your talisman!'

Toby dug into his shirt and brought out a silver disc on a silver chain. The disc was inscribed with a five-pointed star. The wise man waved his fingers and the chain and talisman turned to gold. 'So now you're a wizard, second class,' he told Bat. 'For someone your age that's pretty good going!'

Bat's dark eyes glittered wickedly. 'I'd love to fly Toby and the elephants back to

Feeblerick Hall on a magic carpet!' he said. 'That would give people something to gossip about!'

'You go back by road, the way you came,' the wise man advised. 'People start off gossiping about you using magic, pretty soon a crowd of them come to throw you into prison for it – or even worse! Gently does it!'

'Tell me,' said Bat, 'have you always been wise? Didn't you use magic to get up to mischief when you were my age?'

'Of course not!' said the wise man. 'When I was your age I was perfect . . . an angel!' A glint came into his eyes and he smiled. 'And if you can believe that, you can believe anything!'

FOURTEEN

A Tidy Little Packet

On Monday morning, the villagers of Chewlow looked out of their windows, rubbed their eyes and held their noses. The mound of elephant unmentionables was back in its usual place, steaming away as merrily as a mug of mulled ale.

Councillor Earwacker sprang into instant action and called an emergency meeting of the parish council. Urgent messages were dispatched to Waldo Faldo, Benjamin Thring (the local beadle) and Dan Davies (editor of *The Chewlow Enquirer*). They met outside Councillor Earwacker's house.

'Gentlemen!' the councillor announced like the bell of the church clock tolling midnight. 'The time limit graciously extended to Lady Feeblerick by the parish council has now elapsed and since the elephant pollution problem has not been remedied, it's my duty to see that the law is carried out in a manner that lets me get my own way! I've decided to ask you along as witnesses.'

'An honour, my dear fellow!' gushed Waldo Faldo in a haze of cologne.

'Ho, yuss!' brisked the beadle.

'Earwacker Excels in Elephant Excrement Extravaganza!' cried Dan Davies, scribbling in a notebook.

When the little galaxy of local luminaries reached the main gates of Feeblerick Hall,

they were surprised to find a reception committee awaiting them. There stood Dawkin, looking as disdainful as a cat sniffing at a wedding cake. Beside him stood Toby, wearing a smile that was too big for his face and Bat, who seemed darker and more mysterious than ever. Behind them loomed Rita and Nancy.

'Gentlemen!' said Dawkin. 'Before you proceed any further, m'lady wishes it to be known publicly that she finds herself unable to participate in these proceedings. The whole matter is too indelicate for m'lady's refined feelings. She would like to make it quite clear, however, that she has no intention of handing her elephants over to anyone.'

'But this is disgraceful!' boiled Councillor Earwacker.

'What an old snob!' oozed Waldo Faldo.

'Bit out of order, ain't it?' rasped the beadle.

'Councillor Snubbed by Snob in Too-rude Row!' shouted Dan Davies.

'M'lady has put the whole matter into the horny, but capable hands of Toby Hoken,' Dawkin concluded with a bow so slight as to be a lean.

The deputation from Chewlow turned their solemn eyes on Toby. They looked so serious that the old man laughed like a male voice choir until the tears rolled down his cheeks.

'Hoken!' roared Councillor Earwacker. 'What is the meaning of your raucous levity?'

'It means I got you, Councillor!' Toby tittered. 'I've got the 'ole pack of you prinked, permed and poodle-faked!'

'What do you intend to do about the elephant unmentionables?' bellowed the councillor.

'I'm a-gonna build a little business with it,' said Toby. 'I'm a-gonna take that elephant muck and stick it into sacks stamped "Toby Hoken's Elephant Unmentionables Fertilizer" and then I'm a-gonna sell it. And those 'oo buy it are gonna grow rhubarb as thick as elephants' legs and roses as big as elephants' ears!'

'He'll be famous!' gasped Councillor Earwacker. 'He's going to be a more important man than I am!'

'He's going to make a tidy little packet!' wailed Waldo Faldo, his moustache drooping with disappointment.

'Dosh from dung?' puzzled the beadle. 'Would you Adam-and-Eve it?'

'Hold the front page!' cried Dan Davies. 'Cantankerous Codger Contrives Poo-coup!'

The looks on their faces as they slunk off kept Toby Hoken chuckling for hours.

'Only thing is, lad,' the old man said to Bat confidentially, 'what are we gonna do with all the money we're gonna make? M'lady won't 'ave nothin' to do with it – fertilizer's far too crude for the likes of 'er!'

'Don't worry, Mr Hoken,' Bat replied. 'I'm sure the dwarfs up at Morton Tops could do with some financial help and then, of course,

the elephant house could really do with a heating system for winter.'

'You're right!' said Toby, with a far-off look on his face. 'And then, there's runnin' water, to save us carryin' buckets back and fore and you'll be needin' a little place of your own to live, not to mention . . .'

As Toby's list went on lengthening, Bat felt the soft tap of trunks on his shoulder. He turned around to see Rita and Nancy regarding him anxiously.

'Have those nasty men really gone?' Rita asked.

'What if that awful Waldo Faldo comes back?' shuddered Nancy.

'If Waldo Faldo dares to show his face in Feeblerick Hall again,' Bat declared, 'we'll stick him headfirst in the biggest load of elephant unmentionables we can find!'

Rita and Nancy were so tickled by this idea that they raised their trunks and trumpeted triumphantly.

If you enjoyed this
Mammoth **R**ead try:

The Runner

Keith Gray
Illustrated by Clive Scruton

Jason has had enough of his parents'
arguments. He's running away to stay with
his brother in Liverpool.

On the train journey he meets a 'runner'
called Jam, who lives in the monster
Intercity trains and stations. His carefree
and adventurous life sounds so exciting that
Jason begins to think he might join Jam.

Then Jason discovers Jam's secret . . .

Winner of the Smarties Prize Silver Award
1998

If you enjoyed this
MAMMOTH READ try:

Swapper

Robert Leeson
Illustrated by Anthony Lewis

It was no good going back and saying, 'I've
changed my mind.' No swap backs was
Swapper's rule.

Swapper was for real.

Scott secretly believes he can beat Swapper
and so he begins a massive rolling swap,
trading up day after day, so he can finally
match Swapper and get a Rocket Island.
He takes risks; it seems that anything can
go, including his friendship with Davie.
But in the end Scott realises that some
things are too good to swap and should
be for keeps.

If you enjoyed this
MAMMOTH READ try:

On the Run

Elizabeth Laird
Illustrated by Carrie Herries

In a civil war, who can you trust?

Hania finds an injured freedom fighter and
risks her life to protect him. She must hide
him from her fierce grandfather and from
the military police.

Is Hania a traitor or a hero?